A LITTLE JAMIE BOOK

WHAT SHOULD I WEAR TODAY?

¿QUÉ ROPA ME PONDRÉ HOY?

Little Jamie Books	Los Libros "Little Jamie"
A Day in the Life	Un día en la vida
My Favorite Time of Day	Mi hora preferida del día
On My Way to School	De camino a la escuela
What Day Is It?	¿Qué día es hoy?
What Should I Wear Today?	¿Qué ropa me pondré hoy?

Library of Congress Cataloging-in-Publication Data

Kondrchek, Jamie.
  What should I wear today? / by Jamie Kondrchek; illustrated by Joe Rasemas; translated by Eida de la Vega = Qué ropa me pondré hoy? / por Jamie Kondrchek; ilustrado por Joe Rasemas; traducido por Eida de la Vega. — Bilingual ed.
      p. cm. — (A little Jamie book / Un libro 'little Jamie')
  Summary: A rhyming story in English and Spanish that follows a preschooler through the seasons as his parents help him dress appropriately for the weather.
  ISBN 978-1-58415-839-4 (library bound)
 [1. Stories in rhyme. 2. Clothing and dress — Fiction. 3. Seasons — Fiction. 4. Spanish language materials — Bilingual.] I. Rasemas, Joe, ill. II. Vega, Eida de la. III. Title. IV. Title: Qué ropa me pondré hoy?
  PZ74.3.K665 2009
  [E] — dc22
                                                                            2009025198

Printing   1   2   3   4   5   6   7   8   9

PLB

WHAT SHOULD I WEAR TODAY?

A Little Jamie Book
Un libro "Little Jamie"

STORY BY/POR
JAMIE KONDRCHEK

ILLUSTRATED BY/ILUSTRADO POR
JOE RASEMAS

TRANSLATED BY/TRADUCIDO POR
EIDA DE LA VEGA

¿QUÉ ROPA ME PONDRÉ HOY?

Bilingual Edition English-Spanish
Edición bilingüe inglés-español

Mitchell Lane
PUBLISHERS
P.O. Box 196
Hockessin, Delaware 19707
Visit us on the web: www.mitchelllane.com
Comments? email us: mitchelllane@mitchelllane.com

What should I wear?
  What should I wear?
What's the weather
  like out there?
I look outside
  my window and see
The summer sun shines
  brightly on me.

¿Qué ropa me
  pondré hoy?
¿Hay frío o hace calor?
Miro por la ventana
  y veo
el brillante sol
  veraniego.

4

It's sunny out there,
it's hot out there,
My mother says
that I should wear . . .

Está soleado,
hace calor,
Mi mamá dice
que me ponga . . .

6

A swimsuit, a T-shirt,
   my shorts, and sunblock
Before we go down
   to swim at the dock.

Camiseta, bañador,
   short y bloqueador,
antes de bajar
   al muelle a nadar.

9

What should I wear?
   What should I wear?
What's the weather
   like out there?
I look outside
   my window and see
An autumn breeze blows
   through the trees.

¿Qué ropa me pondré hoy?
¿Hay frío o hace calor?
Miro por la ventana y veo
Que una brisa de otoño
   los árboles agita.

It's windy out there,
it's chilly out there,
My father says
    that I should wear . . .

Está ventoso,
hay frío fuera,
Mi papá dice
que me ponga . . .

A sweatshirt, long pants,
my jacket for fall,
Before I go out to play
with my ball.

*Chándal, pantalones
y chaqueta,
antes de salir a jugar
con la pelota.*

15

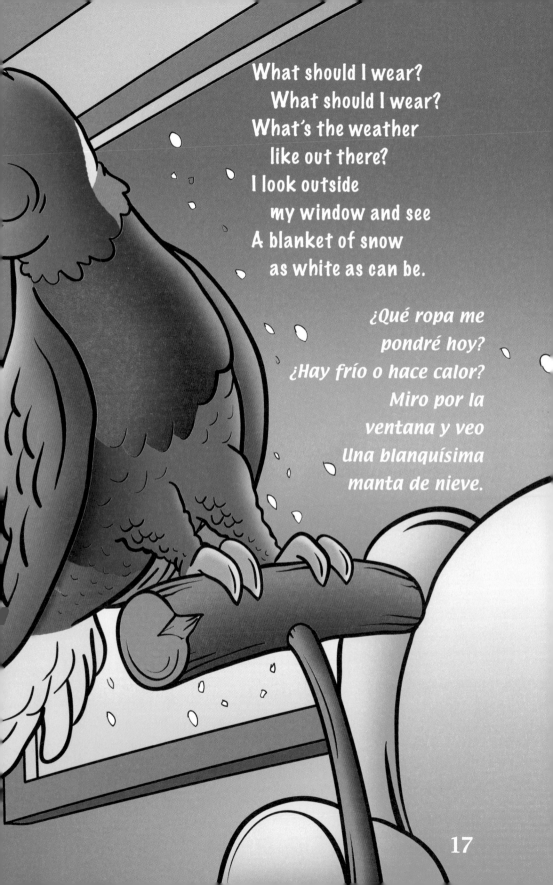

What should I wear?
What should I wear?
What's the weather
like out there?
I look outside
my window and see
A blanket of snow
as white as can be.

¿Qué ropa me
pondré hoy?
¿Hay frío o hace calor?
Miro por la
ventana y veo
Una blanquísima
manta de nieve.

17

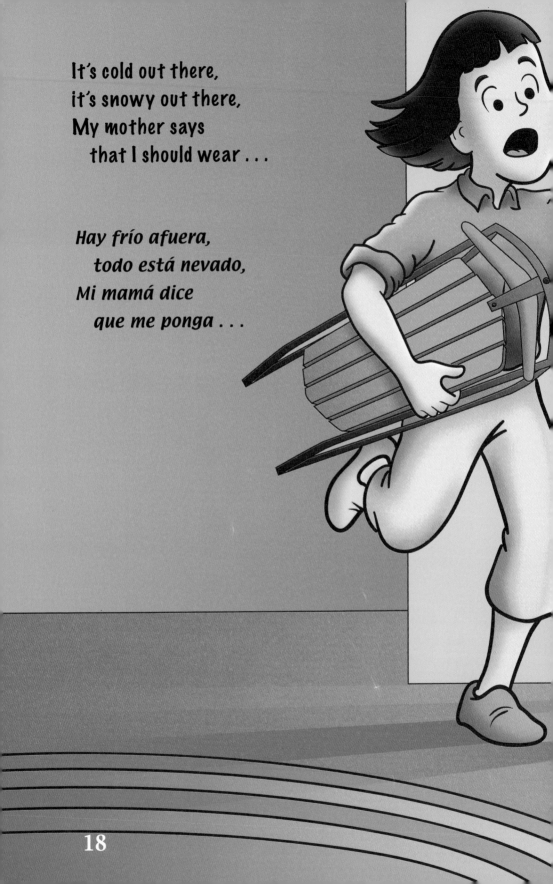

It's cold out there,
it's snowy out there,
My mother says
  that I should wear . . .

*Hay frío afuera,
  todo está nevado,
Mi mamá dice
  que me ponga . . .*

18

19

My coat, my boots,
    a hat on my head,
Before I'm allowed
    outside to sled.

Abrigo, botas, y un gorro
    en la cabeza,
antes de salir a deslizarme
    en trineo.

What should I wear?
What should I wear?
What's the weather like out there?
I look outside my window and see
Spring showers waiting to come down on me.

¿Qué ropa me pondré hoy?
¿Hay frío o hace calor?
Miro por la ventana y veo
Que se acerca un aguacero.

It's rainy out there,
but it's warm out there,
My father says
that I should wear . . .

Fuera llueve,
pero no hace frío.
Mi papá dice
que me ponga . . .

24

A T-shirt, long pants—don't
forget my rain gear.
Splashing in puddles,
I grin ear to ear.

Camiseta,
pantalones,
paraguas y
chubasquero.
Saltando en los charcos,
disfruto del aguacero.

27

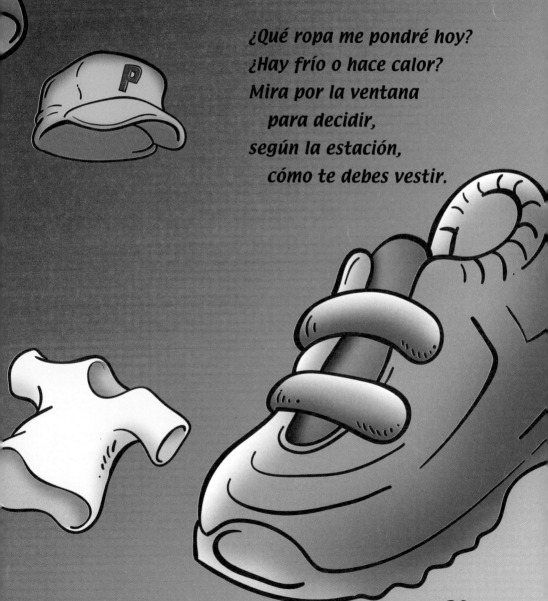
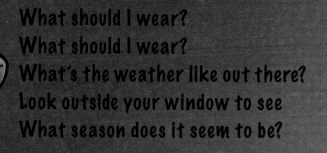

What should I wear?
What should I wear?
What's the weather like out there?
Look outside your window to see
What season does it seem to be?

¿Qué ropa me pondré hoy?
¿Hay frío o hace calor?
Mira por la ventana
   para decidir,
según la estación,
   cómo te debes vestir.

Winter, spring, summer, or fall,
Getting dressed by myself is best of all.
I've clothes for all seasons, no matter the weather.
But today I'll wear clothes as light as a feather!
(What season do you think it is?)

30

Invierno, primavera,
otoño o verano,
vestirse solito es lo mejor.
Tengo ropa para cualquier clima y estación.
La que me he puesto hoy es ligera
como una pluma.
(¿Adivinas la estación?)

About the Author: Jamie Kondrchek earned her master's degree in elementary education from Wilmington University. She has taught pre-kindergarten and kindergarten. Jamie saw the need for read-aloud bilingual books that relate to curriculum standards for this age group. Since these books were often hard to come by, Jamie decided to develop her own collection, Little Jamie Books. She lives in Newark, Delaware.

About the Illustrator: Joe Rasemas is an artist and book designer whose illustrations have appeared in many books and publications for children. He attended Bennington College in Vermont and now lives near Philadelphia with his wife, Cynthia, and their son, Jeremy.

About the Translator: Eida de la Vega was born in Havana, Cuba, and now lives in New Jersey with her mother, her husband, and her two children. Eida has worked at Lectorum/Scholastic, and as editor of the magazine *Selecciones del Reader's Digest.*

JAMIE

JOE

EIDA

Acerca de la autora: Jamie Kondrchek tiene un máster en educación primaria de la Universidad de Wilmington. Ha dado clases de kindergarten y pre-kindergarten. Jamie se dio cuenta de que había necesidad de libros bilingües para leer en voz alta, que se correspondieran con los estándares del currículo para estas edades. Como estos libros eran difíciles de conseguir, Jamie decidió desarrollar su propia colección, Libros "Little Jamie". Jamie vive en Newark, Delaware.

Acerca del ilustrador: Joe Rasemas es un artista y diseñador de libros cuyas ilustraciones han aparecido en muchos libros y publicaciones para niños. Estudió en Bennington College, en Vermont, y ahora vive cerca de Filadelfia con su esposa, Cynthia, y su hijo, Jeremy.

Acerca de la traductora: Eida de la Vega nació en La Habana, Cuba, y ahora vive en Nueva Jersey con su madre, su esposo y sus dos hijos. Ha trabajado en Lectorum/Scholastic y, como editora, en la revista *Selecciones del Reader's Digest.*